Grapefruit Parlor

Ginger Rankin

REBEL
MAGIC

Copyright © 2020 by Ginger Rankin
Published by Rebel Magic Books
www.rebelmagicbooks.com
All rights reserved. No part of this book may be reproduced or transmitted in any form or by any means, electronic or mechanical, including photocopying, recording, or by any information storage and retrieval system, without permission in writing from the copyright owner.
ISBN: 9798648805668

REBEL
MAGIC

Dedicated to
those who are trapped in the web of human trafficking
and those who work tirelessly to free them

Also by Ginger Rankin

Spice Island

Contents

Part One	*11*
1	*12*
2	*16*
3	*23*
4	*26*
5	*28*
6	*31*
7	*33*
8	*35*
9	*36*
10	*40*
11	*41*
12	*44*
13	*47*
14	*49*
Part Two	*53*
15	*54*
16	*57*
17	*59*
18	*62*
19	*64*
20	*70*
21	*71*
22	*76*
23	*79*
24	*82*
25	*85*
26	*87*
27	*90*
28	*94*
A Note from the Author	*97*
Study Guide	*98*
Acknowledgements	*99*
About the Author	*100*

Part One

1

Another bend in the dirt road. I'm not sure this is the right place. It's been so long. I can't feel the ocean breeze from below that always brought with it the smell of salt and decaying fish drying on the shore. I want to look over the rocky edge and see the scuttling, sand-covered Sally Lightfoot crabs sticking their pointed claws into the tiny holes of the lava rock to avoid being pulled back to the sea.

I am getting anxious. If this is the wrong road, then I have spent precious time here for nothing, time I do not have. Looking out at the container ship on the horizon, I slow down a little to see if it is moving at all. Its great bulk picks up the sun and reflects it back to shore. I have watched it so many times as it docks and unloads to fill the store shelves and coolers with poultry, cheese, and butter. It will have machinery that will run the island's construction needs, its spice production and products sold to tourists.

Or am I mistaken? Is it that time has stopped and I am a part of a tableau that has been standing still on this bluff for the last twenty years? Open to a framed still life of painted blue sea and cotton clouds hanging on eight pound test fishing line.

I pause.

No, it's real. And I am here. I'll give it till the next turn up ahead where the road hugs the ridge between the steep bank on the left and the cliff to the right. That's got to be the place.

What people constructed these roads? Did they follow the Arawak trails? Did the Arawak families walk right here where I'm walking, and were their children distracted by the pink frangipani flowers all clustered in the trees? Did they attach the blossoms to their hair and glide like Arawak princesses?

The promised final turn brings me a deep breath of relief. A soft breeze and the salty smell of sea life hits me now. I walk to the edge of the road to peer over the side. At least the sign should still be there. No one would think to carry it off or want to push it further down the steep scarp. Yet I can see nothing. Like this trip from the start, this could turn out to be another stupid idea.

I need to get down to that narrow ledge so I grab onto the exposed root of a sugar apple tree and dig my shoe into the soft loam. I plan my descent to the ledge below. I am sure this is where we dragged the pitch pine boards down.

I remember where we set the foundation wood. I can feel the location now as I would sense my own kitchen if I walked into it blindfolded. I remember we thought the grassy ledge had been put there just for us—a perfect spot, flat enough, and secure against the cliff wall. I look out to sea and recall almost the exact conversation. Our voices are child-like and dreamy.

"Well, look at that. It's a perfect spot!"

"Only if we don't get too close to the—"

"We can't think about that. Let's just do it. Let's get the boards and start to make a floor. We need a floor and a table and a window."

"Where will the window go?"

"In the wall, silly! Come on!"

I can still see Mariposa scramble up the thick web of vines and roots to the road where she turns and waves. The sun is behind her and it imprints her silhouetted chubby figure into my long-term memory. I feel a giggle erupt as I call to her. "Coming!" Then she's gone.

I ease myself to the ledge, high over the rushing waves below. My head is spinning, like a tequila buzz. I don't remember it being so difficult, of course, I was six and fear wasn't an emotion I had welcomed in yet. Suddenly I lose my balance. Pebbles and dirt are skidding past me. I reach for a branch and miss. I can't get a hold on anything and I head straight down. I shut my eyes, as I always do when I feel there's nothing more can be done. I've lost all control and I slide toward the rocks at the edge of the precipice.

Tumbling more, my knees scraping on every jagged rock, I finally stop. I really don't want to see where I am so I keep my eyes shut. Every bone and joint hurts. Slowly peering through squinted eyes, I see that I'm lodged between a log and a jagged board that sticks out of the dirt. There's nothing between me and the sandy beach but forty feet of air. I still have a root in my hand. I lie there shivering in the tropical air and it starts to rain.

If I died here, I wouldn't be found until the weather had eroded my identity. "Body Found. A woman. Looks to be in her twenties. Still holding on to root of custard apple tree she probably thought would save her. No foul play suspected. Investigators will check with tourist office."

How long I will lie wedged between these sharp rocks, looking down at the tempest below, is decided by a slight giving way of the ground and gravel beneath me. There is no option. I grit my teeth and lunge back to the bank. As I do, the large rock I have been leaning against loosens out of place and careens down the cliff without me.

I watch it disappear to a splash, then inch myself up through the thick vines to the road where there are tire tracks and signs of life. A wood sided truck filled with unsecured boulders rattles by on its way up toward the north road. I press my face into the dirt and appeal to any powers that might be available to me to keep the boulders from bouncing off the truck bed and flattening my pathetic gasping self. No energy to move, I shut my eyes again and wait.

2

Why did I come back to this place? Was it just another way to escape? Why escape? Every place I had ever run to was worse than the one I left.

The counselor at the jail in Texas where I spent eight months incarcerated was just a little older than I. She was short and square with a blonde pixie cut. She had been partly responsible for my getting a waiver to attend rehab classes in preparation for release and drug court. Her casual optimism and easy smile in that otherwise bleak place had become my last contact with hope and I hated her. She went home at night. She had two teenage kids who acknowledged her as their mother. To hell with her and her whole family.

Besides, nobody in their right mind, after they knew as much about me as she did, would have a shred of optimism for my future unless they were totally starry eyed. I hated that too, and platitudes, and manipulators. I hated her as soon as she walked into the tiny conference room with its table and two chairs and which, by the way, had carpeted walls, and a camera and microphone set up near the ceiling. Everything I said to her would be on tape. Just leave!

I met with her three times before I even said a word. I only went so I could get out of my cell and away from my whiney cell mate. Each time we met she gave me something to think over for the next time. Homework. As though I would. Nice try.

Since I didn't talk, she did. She laid out her story right in front of me. After week two, I started to get a little interested. She was born in a small town in Indiana and she had both parents until she was an adult. That was good. But it was also bad. Her father abused her mother. He demanded perfection, a spotless house, top grades from the kids, and for them all to be totally submissive. So he beat his wife!

She wanted me to know that no one was perfect. Everyone had a story. She wanted me to know she learned her father suffered from depression and that you can't blame a person for that. I wanted to scream. What a crock!

She said she had finally figured out that lots of people are so filled up with hating themselves that they can't function and so they push it onto someone else. That way nobody ends up happy. So far so good, I thought. Works for me.

She said in the years she'd been a counselor it always seemed to be true.

"So, what's your magic potion?" I asked her.

"We have to learn to care about and love the people we are inside. That way we become strong and confident and more able to make rational decisions."

"Right." I actually snorted.

I felt a little crappy that I did that. She had put up with me for three weeks by now and she was still hanging in. She didn't need to. There's no forcing a counselor to put up with a non-responsive pile of dog shite. Then I felt even worse when I found out she was volunteering her time. And I hated myself even more.

The fifth time we met I resolved to make it worth it for her. It was my last week before parole, release, and drug court. She came in to our carpeted sanctuary and the first thing she did was give me a hug. That was amazingly scary, mainly because you can't do that in there. But she did. She gave me a hug! I could have been cuffed and taken back to my cell to be searched. She could have lost her status as a volunteer and even as a counselor.

I remember standing back and watching the door for a sign that the guards had seen us. The little monitor light was still green and I couldn't hear footsteps or anyone talking. The doorknob didn't turn. No one came bursting in. We cautiously sat down across from each other and I wanted to ask her if she knew how much that hug had meant to me. I had been so disconnected for so long—in fact forever—that her taking the wild chance to hold me meant more than all the words I knew.

There was a sense of urgency to say all the things that needed to be said in this final conversation. I wanted to spill it all, the story of my life, my sense that I had lost the ability to feel, my dark thoughts about suicide. But we didn't have time now. We talked of some practical things like where I was going to stay after my release and who I was going to stay away from, since I was in there for selling some of my drugs on the street and having drug paraphernalia in my back pack. That's it. But if I was caught again, the roof would come down on my head and I'd be back in prison, this time for years.

She had a few notes with her so as not to forget anything. This was the first time I was actually talking and the last time she would see me. She reminded me I needed a plan for re-entry back into the land of the free and home of temptation.

"Can you tell me again what got you into this mess?" she asked, like I could even remember my name at that point.

There were so many reasons. Where did she want me to start?

"I was born." I offered.

She frowned. "I mean this latest mess." I couldn't derail her.

"Oh, that. Yeah." I surprised myself with my brilliant answer. "It was like I was drowning in black muck and I was scared to end it with my razor of choice so when someone handed me some magic pills, I took them."

She didn't seem entirely satisfied with my answer, but she rolled with it, and said, "You thought that you could find the answers to your pain, your bad choices, and your relationships, with drugs."

"And alcohol, don't forget," I interrupted.

"Yes, and alcohol. And you hung with people who couldn't care less about you. You know all this. Is it going to happen again? Do you know how to save yourself from doing that again? Tell me what you've got in your arsenal."

I told her about drug court and that I would have to report every week to my parole officer who was known for a lot of one way conversations, and about the recovery center in town, and staying away from old contacts. She nodded.

"That's good," she gave a quick smile, "that's what other people will be doing for you. You have these ideas and plans in place, and that's important, but can you tell me who this is all for?"

She was trying to work some psychological crap on me and I clammed up. I'd had enough.

"A lot of people are going to care," she said. Then she whispered, "so it's important for you to care, too, or it won't work."

I blanked. It was then that I saw the tear that was making its way down the side of her nose. I handed her the tissue box. This was not easy. She took both of my hands, challenging that damn camera one more time.

"Please try this one thing," she said. "You know we all look at the world through our own lens—our own perceptions. We can change our lens. It's not easy, but we can do it. I'm still working on mine."

I was actually listening to her now for some reason.

She went on. "Please don't be offended but I think you are looking at the world through a lens of fear. You have every reason to do that, given your story, but it makes you sad and kind of stuck. Think back to a time that you felt happy. You own that feeling. It's in there. It's scary to drop your fears at first, but it takes practice to open up to what's possible."

I liked her idea. Every time I thought of a happy time, I thought of this island. I don't know why. I don't remember much about it. It's been so long—this island where my mother, Angel-whoever, gave birth to me. She was young and seriously "not capable," whatever that meant.

I had heard that long after, when I was in my early teens, from my grandmother. She was explaining on the phone to somebody why I was living with her. If that's the case, I come by it biologically. *Not capable*—she had used those words exactly. It's like carrying a big duffle bag around with you from birth, full of dirty socks with holes in the heels. Who wants it? It smells! But you can't shake it.

We learn a lot of things long before we know what words are for. We watch people and see what they do and how they act around us, and that's who we become then, I think. My grandmother didn't want to talk to me about it. She just flat out turned cold on the subject. So I pieced my life story together from bits I heard and some stuff I made up. Depending on the day, it would change. I was a walking delusion.

I lived for a while in a little town called Random, Texas, with my biological mother's mother who didn't talk much except on the phone. She didn't seem to want to admit I was there, except when we ate. Mealtime was important— that and church, and hanging clothes on the line in the back yard, color coded.

On occasion I would get some news indirectly through the cat, Soot. Like when Nama might let slip to Soot that she was going to get her hair done tomorrow and that Soot would be alone pretty much for the day. All that not being true since I was going to be home all day. It was a Saturday. Like I already said, I was invisible. Always.

All that time in Random I felt that I was a bother. And I was. My entire self: my having to get up to go to school, the clothes Nama sewed and hemmed and tucked for me from Aunt Carla's twins, the food I ate—all of it was a bother to her and to the whole universe. And I couldn't find a way to change that.

So, go figure. I am back here on this island that's full of fire ants that are biting me as I lie here waiting to be crushed by boulders and staring at cliffs that call me to jump over the edge. I open my eyes and brush the ants from my bleeding leg. I should probably never have come back.

3

It's not that I didn't try. After jail that time, I set up an appointment with a sliding scale psychologist. She was in a new building connected with the Wellspring Clinic in town. I don't know why I did that; I was free. It must have been the fresh air that got to me. I walked up the stairs instead of taking the elevator, if that tells you anything.

"Anxiety," the receptionist had said. My appointment was on the third floor where the "anxious" people were directed. I was ushered into a tiny room to find out where on the sliding scale my income from cashiering at Foodland would place me for billing.

Then I had to wait until a counselor was ready to tell me, "You have anxiety." She said it with a certainty that I never could have mustered.

"Right," I thought. And I burst into tears. I couldn't stop. I gasped for breath. I wanted to disappear to a dot on a page. She got up, shut the door and sat back behind her desk. I sobbed. I couldn't push down the lump taking shape in my chest.

"Can I get you some water?"

"Oh, yeah," I was yelling now, "water always helps my anxiety!"

So honest to god, she got up and opened the door and left the room to get me a glass of water.

There are ways to stay out of jail but they are not necessarily around when I need them. The rest of my appointed hour went south: tossing water in the counselor's lap, trying to leave, resisting arrest, the white hospital room with handcuffs connected to the bed, and a security guard on a chair outside the door.

My head was swimming in reaction to the injection I received and I finally fell into a sound, snoring sleep. I know that I snored only because I woke up and it was dark and the security guard poked his head in and said, "Jesus, you snore like a freight train."

There comes a point when you just don't care what secrets your body tells when you are asleep, or awake for that matter. But that point is low on the sliding scale of what it's going to take to survive, to breathe one more fricking breath. That's right where I was at that moment. I started to laugh. I lost control. The whole damn thing was hysterical.

A freight train sounded like a good idea. I could imagine sitting in the doorway of an empty boxcar, eating a granola bar, and watching snow-topped mountains passing by. Over there was an occasional buffalo herd, and in the background was the sound of dueling banjos. I fell asleep to the rhythm of the wheels clicking over the rail joints in my head.

All I'd wanted on the third floor of that Wellspring Clinic was to quietly explain to the counselor woman that I was about to welcome my last day on earth with the help of a box cutter razor. I wanted to tell her that my life had been a sweet fucking mess from the day I was conceived, by Angel-whoever, and her invisible male donor. I was taking up space on Earth that didn't belong to me, and now that I understood the situation, I was going to take my leave. I just wanted to tell someone that I was headed out. "So long." But no. She brings me a styrofoam cup full of water. God!

That wasn't the first of my final journeys in and out of my handcrafted hell of a life. By then I seriously hated myself. Not only was I a bother to the planet, but I saw no reason to go on behaving in the same destructive way anymore. And how does one do that? How does one change a lifetime of being a screwup at every turn? At least I realized that! Whatever gifts I had been born with on that tropical island, from Angel-whoever, had been trashed by my inherited incapabilities and my self-generated no-goodness.

After twenty-some years of the high life in the States—and I mean *high* life—I had started to find my highs as easily as you can find a bus stop in Baltimore, although I don't recommend either to anyone.

4

Before I moved in with Grandma Nama and her communications director cat, Soot, in Texas, I had lived here on this island, on and off, with people I can't even name. Those were my first six or so years and I barely remember the time except for a disconnected collection of mind snapshots—some like dim tintypes, and others that were clear color videos. All my memories are separate and alien to each other.

I heard Angel's name spoken at odd times and I was able to piece together a story of my beginning. Angel got pregnant at seventeen. Being from a little Texas town and super religious, her mother—Nama—and father put her on a cruise ship where she cleaned cabins. The timing was perfect, so when the ship got to the island where her sister had moved with her boyfriend, she got off. I was born soon after, at the home of a neighbor who had been trained as a doula. Then my mother left. I was never special to anyone after that.

What I know about my biological mother has frozen my attempts to believe that anyone can ever be a real friend. So I don't look for them anymore. If she couldn't conjure up a bit of love for me as a helpless newborn, I must have had some pretty horrific vibes even then. The worst is not knowing. The silence.

I stayed with a variety of people until I was old enough to enter school and then I was shipped to my grandmother in the States.

My early memories, from zero to six on the island, are a muddled mix. I remember once that I wanted to fly. What better way to release me from my grounded sneakers than to spread my wings and join the geese migrating to exotic worlds, or the yellow butterflies tasting nectar of wisteria in Mexico? Nobody took the time to tell me it wasn't a good idea to fly. No one was around enough for me to check with. I broke my wrist taking off from the house roof with an umbrella. I had a destination in mind other than the backyard. I wore a cast on my arm for a long while and I couldn't do any homework because I pretended I wrote with my left hand. Nobody knew.

5

I had one real friend. In my humble opinion, a real friend is usually a person. Sometimes though it's a dog or even a bug. I heard of a kid who had an imaginary friend named Digger. I'm not sure how that works because wouldn't you be in charge of what an imaginary friend thinks and says? That I wouldn't like, because everything would be going in the same direction. I mean a friend should piss you off once in a while. That's how it was with Mari and me. We used to dare each other to the edge of life itself by holding onto tree-climbing vines and swinging from the side of a cliff into a pool of black at the bottom of a waterfall. Or we would climb to the canopy of a tall island rainforest tree and eat a lunch of mango or custard apple up there. We were always scratched and bruised but we were invincible, and we knew it. Mari is the only friend I ever had.

One Sunday she invited me to come to her church. First, we had to walk to her Uncle Amos' house to get a ride to the north end of the island. We put on dresses and walked through the tunnel to the old town of the island. We shared the tunnel with cars and people and assorted dogs and it was an adventure in itself. We celebrated by yelling our names at the echoing stone walls.

Uncle Amos was a coffin maker. He made them out of pine wood and he carved the name of the dead person on the coffin top by hand. He sometimes carved a flower or angel wings if he had the time.

When we got there, Uncle Amos was in the workshop under his house, planing the wood so the top would fit tight. There were inches of curled wood shavings built up on the floor and around his ankles. The curls were like a little girl's hair on the floor of a beauty salon.

Uncle Amos nodded at us when we entered and said he'd be along in a few minutes. Then I looked at the coffin perched up on the wooden stand where he was working. It was only about three feet long and a foot wide. It was way too small for a real person. I stared at it for a long time until my friend nudged me and said that it was for a little girl who died of dengue fever the day before.

Standing right there in the yellow curls I couldn't move a single part of my body, not even my eyelids. Uncle Amos probably noticed my quizzical look and thought I wanted more information. So he came over to me to explain that he didn't ever waste wood because he always measured the corpse and made the box to exactly fit the body.

I threw up on Uncle Amos' shoes. And then I was so mortified, I ran all the way home without slowing down. I never got another chance to go to my friend's church. That was okay, though. I wouldn't have known what to do when I got there. I did miss the truck ride with Uncle Amos. We were going to sit in the bed of his pickup. We would have shouted at the trees as they sped over our heads and sung *Hail All Hail Sweet Island Home* at the top of our squeaky voices. That would have been another great adventure.

Mari was short for Mariposa, which means butterfly. Mariposa Cielo, Butterfly Sky. I wanted her name so badly, especially after I learned Dolores—me—meant pain. It must have been after that year that the arrangements were made for me to live with Nama and Soot in Random, Texas.

I was going on seven.

6

I wonder if Mari is still on the island. She is so clear in my mind. If I had one picture in my wallet, it would be of her. Her dark eyes and the black afro that she cut herself gave her a baby face. We were direct opposites with my blue eyes and red hair. My rangy body gave no promise of any future athleticism whereas Mari, although a bit chubby, was already muscular and bound for track and field or distance swimming or mountain climbing. She had that look.

Her *who cares* attitude probably got her a long way in making friends and keeping boys in their place. I hope so. I hope she made it through all that adolescent crap and craziness that happens to us girls like clockwork.

Even today I don't seriously try to find her. Oh, if somebody would say, "Hey, remember Mariposa? I heard she's teaching at Harvard," I would be over the moon for her. But the chances being what they are, I don't want to hear otherwise. I have her in my heart and that's working okay.

She was smart. She had a kind of natural knowing. Even at seven years old she knew not to touch the Jumbie Umbrellas—poison mushrooms—that popped up after the rain. She warned me that they only grow in dark places and they hold evil people's spirits after they died. Some people eat them—not Mari and me though. I've seen recipes in books but they look like that crepe you put on your door when someone's dead. *Mushroom* comes close to the way I feel about them. Rooms full of mush.

Mari and I spent whole days playing together. After her, I never had anybody real to be with. Everybody I met later was trying to get something from me. Nobody ever again wanted to just laugh and explore and almost kill themselves jumping from the top of a waterfall with me.

7

When I was sent to live with Nama I had to register at another school. I was put back in first grade and I got to school by a yellow bus. The bus started and finished every single weekday like a bad dream that I accepted as if it was nasty medicine. To be new in school with kids who have been together since kindergarten is a job for a more confident child than I was.

I had no natural equipment to use, no glib or colorful responses to nail them with, no way to stop the tears that came to my eyes when they picked up their things and moved away from me at recess. I dreamed of having a talent that I could wow! the class with like having that one voice the whole class turned to look for when we sang the *Star Spangled Banner*. But I had no skills that would impress the little critics seated in their first grade chairs around me or climbing the monkey bars outside at recess. My clothes had all attended the same classes in years past, on the hodgepodge bodies of Aunt Carla's kids. So expectations were pretty low for me ever being part of the group or even allowing myself to feel like I cared.

To add to it, I didn't understand half of what the teacher said but I was too afraid to ask questions. I'll give her credit for starting out by seeing that I got the books and papers I needed and introducing me to the class. She charged a perky little blonde girl to be my social connector for the first few days but Amy lost interest in me on day two and moved back with other whispering witches where she fit in better.

I was in my element though. Throughout my short life I had never felt anything other than a misfit and a nuisance, except when I was with Mariposa So the whole experience was totally expected. As things go then, it's not strange for me to find myself now, at age twenty-seven, face down in the dirt on a tropical island. Where else would I be?

8

I pull myself up from the gravel by the road, little stones and sticks imbedded in the palms of my hands. Brushing myself off and finger-combing my hair, I decide to walk into town to the *Ruby Inn* where I already have a space rented. I can take a shower and decide what to do with the two days I have left. If I'm lucky, no one will see me before I can make an assessment of my bruises and cuts in the privacy of my own room.

I'll come back to the cliff again. There are a couple of things I've promised myself before I take the plane back to Texas and the end of my story.

I mark the custard apple tree. It looks like all the others along the road, so I also drag a rotting log from across the way and prop it up at an angle and I pull my scarf from my pocket and tie it to a broken branch. Now I'll see it from the bus tomorrow on my last visit to the *Grapefruit Parlor*.

We had settled on the name *Grapefruit Parlor* since there were always ripe grapefruits available for the taking under the citrus trees all over the place. We planned to construct a wooden roadside stand, squeeze the grapefruits, and sell the juice in little cups to travelers on the road to town. If we were lucky, some of the tourist vans would make us a regular stop. We would become known all over the island. That was the plan.

I would find the spot again tomorrow, but meanwhile in the darkening, I needed to go.

9

The walk was long and the silence needed to be filled so my brain started its manic screaming at me. It does this occasionally but I had hoped that being on this tropical island with the velvet breeze, it would have given it a rest. But no. The slide show of my life clicked on and I had the only seat in front of the screen watching my greatest shit storms.

They had etched themselves in pretty deeply. In one, I was in sixth grade and the teacher assigned us to research a famous person. It had to be someone who had done good for the world in some way. This was to inspire us to have goals and heroes. We were to give her suggestions and she would write them on the board. We had all the usuals, like Eli Whitney, Betsy Ross, and Abraham Lincoln.

She made the decisions about who was acceptable, so it was *No* to the Lone Ranger, Frodo, Gandalf, and Snow White. It took ages to get through that part. Some of the kids fought for their own heroes. It especially took time when two or three wanted the same person.

I picked Mr. Rogers. He was the only person I ever related to who was famous and he did lots of good things for people. I thought so, anyway. We had a week to prepare. We had to present a speech to the class the following Friday, and we also had to look like our celebrity.

I was a tiny bit interested in this project. At least I was going to give it a go. I had never spoken in front of more than one person at a time but I put that part out of my mind. I went to the library to find all the books on Mr. Rogers. There weren't any books on him so I thought I'd just watch his show every afternoon after school and make up the rest.

Getting off the bus that day I was thinking about the report and I settled in to watching *The Neighborhood* right away. Nama and Soot were in the kitchen canning peaches so I didn't have to explain why I was watching a baby show and not reading a book. I curled up on the couch and put a blanket over my head. I felt like I was in a proper home. I wasn't sure what 'home' felt like but I knew that I was warm and comfortable. I became aware of my slow breathing and when Soot came in and jumped up and wanted to nuzzle under my arm, I fell asleep in home heaven.

When I woke up the news was on and Soot was crying to go out the front door. I'd missed the whole Monday Mr. Rogers and I had only three more days to write my Portrait of a Famous Person.

Those days went by fast, along with my enthusiasm for the assignment. I found myself AWOL during the Mr. Rogers' show for a variety of reasons on Tuesday, Wednesday, and Thursday of that week. I'm not stupid. I knew it was still due on Friday. I could feel the buzz building up in the classroom with kids bringing in their costumes, hats, beards, and storing them in the front closet. The less I prepared the more stupid I thought the whole idea was.

The teacher told one kid he had to wait for Friday to bring in his bloodhound. He was portraying the Russian scientist Ivan Pavlov and was going to show the class how his dog drooled at the sight of a piece of cooked chicken. I knew a bloodhound didn't need anything to get him to drool. I'd been at a house once that had a hound named Cosmo, and we all had to dive out of the way every time he shook his head so as not to be slathered with his spit.

I'll get to the point. I never made an excuse for not being ready for my report. True, I didn't have anyone helping me with it or with a costume, but it was my stupid fault. Thursday night I stayed up late and wrote a couple of paragraphs about a generic person on television who was very nice and made you feel good because he liked you for no other reason than because you were you. That sounded so soppy and pathetic I almost tore it up, but then I would not have had anything to say and I'd just stand there in Nama's husband's old sweater she'd kept after he died. It was blue and grey and too big for me but, oh well.

Friday came. Probably on my list of top five worst days of the approximately four thousand I had lived up to that point, give or take. We listened to Abraham Lincoln, Princess Diana, and Eleanor Roosevelt. We had recess and I came after that.

Making my way to the front of the room I was at first stunned that I had forgotten the sweater. It was at home on my bed. I could see it in my mind, lying there, blue and grey. What I had left was the two pukey paragraphs.

I need to say that this was so typical of me that I almost felt like grinning from the familiarity of it. Nothing new here. I can only think now that I had done this to myself on purpose. I wouldn't have known that then but it was what I later learned was self-sabotage. I blew myself up on a regular basis. Why I did that is clear. I hated myself like you would hate a rat that ate through your lunch bag and finished everything down to the fruit roll. I didn't know at the time why I despised myself but later it was explained to me many times. So when I read the first paragraph aloud and I heard a muffled snicker from the side of the room, I dropped my paper and turned around and I mooned the class. Literally. They deserved it. I deserved it. We all deserved it, including the teacher who ushered me out of the morgue-silent room and down to the principal's office.

I heard hints that there were several options discussed for me in the teachers' room that day. Most of the teachers wanted me gone—moved to the other middle school—that very day. Others wanted to think about it over the weekend and decide on Monday. The students were a mixed bag. Some piously felt I had crossed the line of decency and decorum and came close to destroying their entire middle school experience. Others thought it was so funny they couldn't look at each other at lunch without snorting milk out their noses.

There was lots of pretending that nothing happened. No one talked to me, as usual. I would forever be the girl who pulled down her pants and showed her butt in Mrs. Larkin's sixth grade room. It shocked even me when Mrs. Larkin quieted the class after lunch by saying that we all make mistakes. She went on to hope that if we didn't hurt anyone, the mistakes would soon be forgotten. I still wonder if that was a first at Hemlock Middle School. It caused some excitement in an otherwise predictable day, after which we went on with portrayals of famous people, part two.

10

I wonder at my ability to stay out of jail as long as I did. Until I was nineteen. I felt every day like I was living on the wrong planet. Someone had made a big mistake and let me on anyway. There was no way out except the obvious, which I tried when I was arrested the first time for drinking underage and throwing beer bottles at a liquor store window. I still have the scar on my wrist from a Corona bottle shard I used to slit my vein. Obviously it didn't work, but I was a step closer to knowing how it was done.

11

Walking down out of the dense trees, the road opens up to the town where I'm staying. Lights are on in the main street that runs along the edge of the sea. The box where the traffic cop used to climb up the steps to stand and direct traffic has been transformed into a street lamp, but I can still see him there. One sleeve of his uniform was white. That was the arm to watch. It directed the cars up the hill, around the roundabout, and off to market hill. It was the same white sleeve that hurried all the walkers in their various directions as the vehicles waited. We called him the Cop in the Box. The new light doesn't come close to giving you the same confidence. Nor does it wink or wave.

The air is still hot and the heat bounces up off the tar road. It's dark now so I pass the inn and walk down to the levee and sit with my feet in the water. Night in the tropics. A cruise ship horn blares for the second time. There will be one more signal to call everyone aboard and onto the next adventure. The sound is both familiar and haunting.

As a little girl, I used to wonder what happened on that big boat. It made the town shrink when it eased up to the Carenage, where the tall ships used to come years ago to avoid careening over in surprise nighttime storms.

These days the ships are without billowing sails. They don't carry precious metal or raw materials or shanghaied slaves. They don't come across wild oceans full of pirates who board their decks and abscond with their cargo, leaving sailors adrift or dead.

These were cruise liners filled with pleasure seekers, lovers, the gregarious and the shy, and some hungry for a moment away from a life that had no windows for their souls. I could be wrong, but that's who I saw filing on and off, when I got close enough.

What was dinner like for them? I imagined long tables of food, lots of melons cut like baskets and lobsters with their tails cooked red, and sizzling steaks on separate grills, with chocolate cakes and rainbow ice cream. There wouldn't be one thing there that didn't make my mouth water.

When I think back to plates of food in my childhood, they mostly held mashed breadfruit and chicken back soup, with roti to dip in it. We went around with crocus sacks and picked up the fruit from the ground around the trees and cut it up in a bowl to share. Funny how clearly I can see those dinners from so long ago.

I feel an old smothering sadness. I can see the people pile out of the vans that have taken them to the sights on the island. I know the stops by heart. There is the English fort with its wrought iron cannons and secret passages underneath that wound maze-like until they emerged underwater. There is the deserted sugar plantation, the botanical gardens, the volcanic lake in the center of the island with its diminishing number of howler monkeys, and the red brick parliament building. I know them all. I must have walked the island a million times with Mari.

The sadness is familiar—it crouches in my mind, always ready to leap. Always. I am covered up in it as I sit on the dock. For a while I think I'll change my flight and go back to Texas tomorrow, a day early. But it will incur a fee and I have my money figured to the penny. My head starts to pound. I feel lost. I could end this now, I think. Walk to the end of the grey splintered fishing dock and silently slip into the quiet black water. No one would know. No one would even wonder.

12

The white cruise ship will sail soon, in the dark night, to the next island. I watch the querulous tourists gather from all parts of the island. Some reddened from too much sunbathing, others disappointed, tired, and hungry. I still can't understand them. They swarm like swallows to a place they have never been and blanket it with their curiosity. They want to fill their pockets with odd objects, and their memory banks with incidents to show and tell to those who haven't been so fortunate to travel. Do they come to learn or to compare? Maybe to criticize.

I watch as the last of them climb the gangplank and enter the glittering ship. They are more than likely offered a tray of rum drinks, compliments of the island, and then reminded that a formal dinner will be served in the main dining room in two hours.

The van drivers in the car park cluster and discuss their day. They will be taking this opportunity to unwind and share their stories: the couple who insisted on the front seat behind the driver and never stopped relating their past travels, safaris, and icy trips to Greenland; the woman who tried to get the other passengers to sing *The Wheels on the Bus*; and the several who wondered why they even got off the ship at this island since they "are all so much alike" and the earrings they bought were "made in China, for god's sake." The local drivers laugh and know that tomorrow is another Sunday and another ship. The vans grind to a start and head home.

What is home? Where is home? I leave the edge of the dock and walk toward the fast darkening street. The inn's gas lamp is flickering by the door that has been left unlocked. Ruby is in the kitchen when I enter.

"What in the world?" Her eyes pop wide when she sees me.

"I'm fine, I just tripped on some branches on my walk." I work up a smile.

"Oh, darlin', you ain't fine. Look at you." She grabs a wash cloth from the folded laundry pile, wets it in the sink and hands it to me.

"Here, dab this on your face. Sit down on this chair. Oh Sweet Jesus, help us out here."

I laugh. Nobody ever freaked out over me getting bloody before and I never knew what it would be like. It feels funny. I put my head down on the table and laugh so hard it turns into a long sob. I feel Ruby's arms tight around me and we stay that way a while until my heart slows down and I catch my breath. I could stay like this forever. Ruby whispers in my ear that things are going to be all right and do I need a doctor because she can call her brother from Grand Bay.

"No, no doctor, I'll be okay. Just need a shower and then a little sleep."

I look up and Ruby has a warm chicken roti on a plate and a glass of milk set in front of me. I love the delicious little wraps with chicken meat inside. I can smell the curry sauce and my tears start to flow again. I'm in heaven this time for real.

After I finish the roti and milk, Ruby asks me to tell her what's happened. She says she has all the time I need. I weigh whether or not I can put my thoughts together, and decide that I may never get another chance to get my story out into space.

I always felt that there was a place out in the earth's atmosphere where everything was stored and never lost. I have lots of stuff out there, some of it is pretty awful and scary. It's a childish thought, but it could be true. I never got rid of the idea that my crazy stupid life would someday be retrieved and somebody would be able to sort through it and put it into some order. It might even be helpful for someone else. Wacky, I know.

13

Hours later in my bed, with mosquito netting surrounding me, I wonder what Ruby thinks of me. She'd asked for my story but I don't think she was prepared for the weight of it. She was quiet through it all. She drank herb tea and listened without saying a word. I couldn't read her.

When my voice fell and I said, "That's my story," she reached over and put her hand on my cheek and then stood up and said, "You need your rest. You have a big day tomorrow."

My story had come out in that small kitchen with its windows open to the soft tropical air. I had started at the very beginning: a mother who had sex with an unknown quantity and gave birth to a baby girl. Instead of all the other choices she had, she decided to dump the baby and sail away. She had no proof or thought of what would happen to that kid.

What kind of a person can leave a tiny new life like that? I have always wondered which genes allow a person to be so inhuman. I can't help but despise her. How much of my disaster life is her fault? I don't like to whine but I guess I did, there in Ruby's kitchen.

I went on about my drug life and jail time, the domestic abuse I suffered because I couldn't walk away. I had thought he was right to beat me. I probably deserved it. Who wouldn't want to take his frustration and hate out on me since it was probably all my fault anyway, like he said. Ruby doesn't count. She just came in at the end and didn't have to be around me long. Even if she liked me for a little while she would soon realize that she was wrong and back off.

I'm only here to finish off my plan. I'll go back to the road tomorrow.

14

I finally fall asleep and it is deep and still. The blackness of the room and the netting around the bed encourage me to go back under each time my eyes open or my consciousness rises to waken.

Slowly, through a fog, I see a jeweled castle on the sandy floor at the nethermost part of the ocean of my dream. Its outer walls are set with green emeralds and the turrets are iced with white diamonds. I recognize it immediately as the home of Ariel and her father king Triton, her five sisters, and her grandmother. It is one of two videos on my Nama's shelf that I watched so many times I had it memorized.

But now it is before me in glorious swaying reality, and I am there, in the ancient fairy tale, swimming in and out of the open windows, through the bedrooms and the golden reception hall. I can rise to the mosaic ceilings and drop to the cut stone floors inscribed with gold inlay stories of former royalty and their exploits and triumphs.

I loved that Ariel was the youngest of five daughters. They were mermaids. They could live three hundred years if they would do it with tails instead of legs. The sisters could see the benefit of tails rather than legs. They didn't need to walk. They had a great life. But Ariel, when she turned fifteen and was given the choice to rise to the surface of the sea, was dazzled by the views and the sky and especially by a young royal sailor she saw having his birthday celebration on the deck of a ship. They were all dancing and not paying attention to a huge wave that was coming straight for their ship. When the wave hit, it swept the handsome prince from the slick boards and over the rail into the water. In my dream I feel the need to reach out to him just as Ariel had done.

Anybody can guess the rest, I suppose. Ariel rescues the prince and they live happily. But it's more tangled than that, with Ariel having to give up her mermaid tail to acquire legs so she can live on land. Not only that but she gives up her family and the precious studded castle and her three hundred years of certain life to become human, convinced it will be a better deal. She gets a prince, pretty gowns, legs, and eventually gets to die and go to heaven. She decided this without any counseling or psychological testing. I, for one, think she was insane to forfeit life in the sea for all the problems that come along with being human.

There are a lot more complications. But let's just put it out there again. Ariel wanted legs, a handsome husband, cool clothes, the promise for albeit a shorter life, *and* the chance to go to heaven. I've rolled this over in my mind so many times. And for all of this she drank a potion stirred up by an ugly witch who took her precious singing voice away from her into the bargain.

This tale is hundreds of years old. Every so often someone comes up with an altered version but it's always the same at its core. You want more than what you have? You're not happy with who you are? Do I have a deal for you! All your answers are in this little beige pill. Take this one on the house. I have plenty more. And yes, you'll have to pay. But that comes later. Don't worry about it now.

I feel my body shaking as I swim by the villainous sea witch Ursula and she reaches out to grab my trailing net gown, missing by inches. She holds a hollowed coral cup filled with a potion she has made especially for me.

"Here you are my sweet. I've heard your story. You deserve to be happy."

I swim faster, without looking back, but then she reappears right in front of me. I know the ending to this horrible tale: I take the little beige pill and drink it down with the black potion and then I belong to her. I know this because I have been through this many times before in my own life.

My whole body begins to shake. This isn't a dream. This is how my life is going to end, right? When I turn the page, it's going to be blank.

Part Two

15

When I open my eyes, the ceiling is turning like a vinyl record. I'm wrapped in the mosquito netting and my sheets are damp. I would believe it if someone tells me I've been to the bottom of the sea. Holding onto the four-poster bed keeps me from sinking to my knees as I inch over to the door, where Ruby now appears.

"Hi, I'm glad to see you're up." She moves toward me.

"I'm so sorry, Ruby." I'm still wearing the mosquito netting like a bridal veil and the sheets are caught up in my feet. "I'm a total wreck."

"You're okay. Not everyone would look so good in those duds." She smiles.

I actually smile back. "I'll wash these up and get going. You've been—"

"No, I have someone who'll do that. You go on and take care of your day."

Tomorrow's flight back to the States leaves at 9am. I'll call for a van driver later, one who doesn't mind a quick trip to the airport rather than waiting in line for a gaggle of cruise travelers. But today is Saturday and that means market day. I shower and dress.

Saturday market always stirs up this little island country. There are many more people meandering out in the streets than on other days. Joining the moving crowd is exactly what I need now. We step in rhythm to the music coming from the car windows. The air is filled with the grilling of fried bakes and coal pots heating the lambi and rice with plantains. The smells spark blurry pictures in my mind that come into focus as I move through the colorful skirts and shirts and wrapped head scarves.

A bright woven basket filled with fruit and handmade dolls is balanced on the head of a woman weaving her way to her booth, children clinging to both her hands. Mango juice runs down the chin of the smaller child and drips onto her blouse. She looks down and flicks at it and goes on sucking the fleshy seed.

"Think of a time you were happy," Holly had said, "a time when you laughed and felt good about yourself." We were in the carpet-walled room. I was in my orange jail suit. "You own those feelings, you know. They're yours anytime you decide you want them back," she'd said.

Happiness is sucking on a rich ripe mango and letting the juice run down your chin. Why not?

Over where the vans park in the market there is a car with its trunk open. Inside there are trays of freshly made bread pudding. I know the cook had risen before dawn to stir together the rich mixture and bake the pudding in an outdoor oven before she packed it into her car and traveled the long winding road to market. This is her gift to the island. It's her entire income. I buy two squares for myself to eat right there, and a paper plateful to carry back to Ruby. She will appreciate the thought.

Leaving the plate of bread pudding in the refrigerator for Ruby, I hope she loves it as much as I do, with its hint of nutmeg and cinnamon.

I go to my room and see that the bed net is back up and the sheets are on the bed. Everything is in order. All I need is to change to jeans and hiking shoes, and grab my little hand shovel and burlap crocus bag of miscellaneous tools. What else will I need on this final lap of my journey before I head back to the States?

16

The online boarding pass for tomorrow has me seated in row 23 on the aisle as it flies north. I will land in Abilene and ride the bus to Random. Nama moved into a home for seniors two years ago. She sold her house and is using the money she received for her assisted living apartment. Soot died before she had to think about making arrangements for him.

I don't know why I am going back to Random except that it's what I know. I'll have a first floor apartment in a duplex house with a small front yard and no garage. No one seems to have a garage in Random. Most of the houses are decades old and rely on attached breezeways with just enough of a roof to keep the golf ball hailstones from denting their decades old cars.

I honestly haven't found what I was looking for here. For a while I thought that Holly, the volunteer counselor at the jail, had been onto something. Her excitement and her experience had stirred me to reach outside my cocoon to think I might grab onto a new kind of life. But my thoughts are clouded again standing here with the bright sun beating down on me.

I feel I have looked everywhere for reasons to go on. All of the potions I have taken, the advice, the books, and the mind-bending, self-appointed television preachers, haven't cured my hollow feeling. I still feel detached from any purpose in living.

I often envision an old balancing arm scale with nature on one side and nurture on the other. No weight registers on either side on my scale—no nature and definitely no nurture. I wonder who I am and where my story is.

17

I take a van to the place along the road where the ledge is located. As it swerves around the unprotected corners, I shut my eyes and tell myself that if we are going to fly over a cliff it will be a very quick way to go.

The other folks jammed in beside and around me have a look of resignation. I practice that look. It involves a somber, pondering kind of face and sometimes the closing of one's eyes to convey that your thoughts are far away and not about whether the bald front tire blows or the next bend in the road hides a washout from last night's rain. It will take me a while to be good at that look.

We take a sharp turn by the cemetery before my stop. I think of Mariposa and her Uncle Amos, the coffin maker. There's a wrought iron gate at the entrance of the graveyard. Another blurry picture shakes me. It was here at this gate that Mari and I had stood and watched the lighting of the graves. It was All Hallows' Eve and we had gone down with Mari's mom. She was a small energetic woman who made me feel like a second daughter. She rarely stopped talking, but when she did stop, she moved into humming spirituals. I never knew when to say something since she always had something going on.

All over the cemetery and as far as one could see, the graves had people sitting in circles around them. They held lit candles with umbrellas above them so the flames wouldn't go out. The flames flickered through the waterproof umbrellas making the burying ground look like it was planted with big lighted mushrooms.

We must have been very young. It was all a mystery to me. A giant of a man stood at the gate in denim jeans and jacket. He wore a blue denim hat with a wavy brim and he moved in a slow circular dance. With his arms raised, he looked down at us and in a deep song like voice said, "Welcome to the party of the dead."

I don't remember being afraid at all. It was like a party. No one was crying. Later I asked what was happening and found out that they were just honoring their dead, some recent and some ancestral. "Welcome!" and "Party!" stuck with me. How different from my concept of death today as a deep, dark, and unknowable place that some people leap into and are never talked about again.

Someone had handed me a little folded paper cup with hard parched corn ground up with a little sugar thrown in. It was called asham. It was made in memory of those who were no longer here. It had tasted sweet and mysterious like I expected it would.

I mainly remember that I was in a place where I could have been scared out of my skin. Why wasn't I? Inside I was confident and curious. Being so young, what was it I sensed then?

The van finally stops. Working my way around the seats to the open door, I pay the conductor and step out into the heat of the day. He jumps back inside and takes off flying, with the load of islanders jostling and bobbing inside.

There it is, my custard apple tree with my scarf tied to the log leaning against it, but minus part of the root that had probably saved my life. There are the skid marks from my

60

shoes heading down the embankment toward the edge of the cliff. There's the ledge that Mariposa and I had discovered. Reaching it is easier this time.

I rummage around the ground hoping to find one thing, anything that would have lasted from our adventure two decades before. I dig with my little hand shovel like an archaeologist, grateful for the breeze from the ocean below.

I should have made it here earlier. I forget that, so close to the equator, the sun goes down quickly and with no apologies at 6pm every day.

I lift a flat rock and see part of a plank beneath it. It's under so much eroded soil and networks of vines that it never would have been found if not for my searching. My heart thumps as I uncover more of it. It is finally loose enough to see that it is about four feet long. It was a reject from Uncle Amos' coffin shed because of the big knothole in the center. No one wanted to be buried in a coffin with a hole that big in it, or any holes for that matter. He said we could have it and what did we want it for? "Oh," we had said, "just a sign."

18

I grab the edge of the board and pull at it. It finally gives a little. More digging. I don't want to break it, for lord's sake. Up it comes unbroken with dozens of ants, rolly-pollys curling up into balls for protection from the air. Centipedes and bugs I do not know, are scattering from their quiet dark existence to another safe place.

I turn the board over and there it is—GRAPEFRUIT PARLOR—in finger-wide, shaky letters made from cotton dipped in indigo dye from Uncle Amos. He had no idea what sign we were about to create when he handed us the tuna can. It had a quarter inch of the rare dye out of the generosity of his heart. He warned us not to drop it since there could be no more.

I've found our sign! I carry it gently and lean it against where I think our planned travelers rest stop had been. It had taken a bit of thinking and compromise to come to a decision about what we were actually doing there. Mari and I often had plans that only gelled toward the end of our efforts.

For instance, the discarded batik scarves we were given had to remain scarves and not the princess gowns we had designed. We were not allowed to use the scissors that Mari's Auntie Del used for her fine quilts. Neither could we sew, because we simply didn't know the first thing about it.

There were so many things we planned that never materialized. The delight was in the ideas, the drawings in the sand, the eloquent description of our dreams. That made up our days from morning to night.

But the Grapefruit Parlor came closest to really happening.

19

I pick up the board and set it up against the bank. GRAPEFRUIT PARLOR.

As I look for a dry place to sit a while, before I leave, I hear a small voice.

"Where've you been?"

I squint into the shady recess where the bushes hang down loaded with wilding guava. I don't expect to see anything but something's there. I decide to accept this offering as if from my mind and pursue it wherever it takes me. I'm not apprehensive. I breathe deep and let it go.

"I know, I should have come back sooner," I whisper. "Where have *you* been? What have you been up to?"

"Here, waiting for you! We have so much to do. Oh good, you brought the sign." The voice is familiar and sweet, like singing.

I look around and see that nothing has changed from the first time I had seen this place with Mariposa. But the voice is not hers.

"Come on, help me set up this wall. We can't serve juice to customers if we don't open our doors. I brought a box of grapefruit a while ago but it doesn't last forever, especially when it's already ripe on the ground. I'll have to get more, and some cups. Running a juice parlor is more work than we thought but we can do it. It'll just take a bit more time."

How do I tell her I'm not staying? I put my head down on my knees for a minute. My mind is spinning with versions of how to say "I'm leaving tomorrow, forever." But she has already caught my drift.

I know she heard me thinking because she says, "Oh that's okay. I wasn't sure that you'd be able to stay. You're grown up now. Probably have a million things to do." And then "I'm just glad you made it back for a little while at least. I have so many things to tell you. But wait, I want you to see this."

I move over near the guava bush and there on the ground is a land snail. You know the ones that look like a spiral shell with a little body tucked inside. I bend down to see the creature.

"It's a gastropod," she says. "I'm so glad you got here before I took her out and let her go in the moss. I think she must be about to lay eggs. She's pretty big and probably has stopped growing now."

"How do you know all this?"

The voice takes on an eye rolling sound. "If you watch, you learn."

"Oh, yeah, I remember," I hear myself murmur.

She goes on. "Do you know, if she lays eggs they'll hatch out into tiny, already made snails, with miniature spiral shells just like hers? Then they will slither on their own mucous right off by themselves and find food and start to grow and have a family too. And do you know they eat with a mouth? Look!" She holds it up under my nose.

It's a snail, all right. I try to be excited.

"Look closer at it," she insists. "It started out tiny like the middle of her shell and then she kept growing swirls of shell, each one bigger as her body grew. See? Now look just below her feelers. That's where her mouth is."

I have to think when I've ever seen a snail so close that I could follow its corkscrew shell from the center to the round opening where its head poked out, and watch its antennae searching around. "Does she have eyes?" I ask.

"You're lookin' at them!" She laughs. "They're stuck right on the end of her feelers. She's actually lookin' at you. See?"

Mesmerized, I stare at this wee miracle.

"There's more you know," she says.

I look in the direction of the voice. "Really?" I say it sarcastically because by now I am sure that none of this is real. It's a daydream or one of those weird conversations a person has with themselves when they are drowsy or drugged or beyond drunk. I've had them before, of course.

"Yes, there is and you should listen to this with both your ears."

"Oh, my god, this is crazy. Okay, okay, I'm listening."

"Good, because Delia has to leave soon."

"And her name is Delia because?"

"Because I named her. It's short for Cordelia. But Cordelia is a sad name because she is killed in a play so I shortened it to Delia. In Celtic, Delia means Daughter of the Sea, like Ariana. Remember her? Anyway, she doesn't have all day."

I'm not sure but I think that is all said in one breath. The voice goes on.

"Now, Delia is a land snail. She would drown in the water just like you would if you fell into the sea and couldn't swim. She can't swim either. She'd go right to the bottom. So, here's the thing. She stays on land in her little shell of a house and if water comes up to her door or anything else that would be dangerous to her, she first checks in with herself, then she pulls back into her house and shuts the door made of mucus that she's built just for such occasions. She's like us. She wants to be alive. She wants to be happy and mush around in the moss and eat algae and mushrooms and an occasional wild strawberry. She is curious to see what's around the next bend in the road. And she carries her home with her, so wherever she finds herself she's at home."

"Okay, Mariposa!" I'm smiling. "It's you, isn't it? Come on out." I go to the guava bushes and shake them till some of the fruit drops to the ground.

Silence. I am alone with myself. But the voice was real. It was.

I walk to the edge overlooking the cliff. The lowering sun is creating evening colored ripples on the water below. The tide is still. It looks like it is deciding which way it will roll, as if there ever was a chance it might change its mind.

And what if that could happen? What if we are going along all our lives in a direction believing all those things that have happened to us in the past have the power over what we do next. Then, we get to wondering what would happen if we'd choose another path? What is the possibility life would be worse? Better? It really couldn't hurt to try so long as you're careful and don't knock anyone over in the process—just let go and, *bingo*, a new possibility. Why not?

Still holding Delia, I bring her level to my eyes. I have never talked to a snail before, but I suspect that this will not be the last time.

"Well Delia, you're a pretty wise gastropod." I move over to the rocks at the base of the bank, careful to keep her centered on the palm of my hand.

"It's interesting to meet you eye to eye, my friend. And carrying your home with you is really a brilliant idea, isn't it?"

I place her on the softness of the thick moss. She'll know what to do now. She has business to take care of. All those eggs to lay.

I turn and grab onto a likely vine and pull myself up to the road and shake myself off.

"You own those feelings," Holly had said. "If you've ever felt happy, or confident, or even brave, you can feel that way again, you know. It's yours to choose."

Just then a van comes behind me and slows down. "Ride into town, Miss? Save you time!"

I swing onto the running board and weave myself back to the only open seat. The child next to me is returning home from school. He has a full backpack and wears a uniform of khaki shorts and white shirt. A six year old, in primary school, I guess. His sleepy head keeps rolling back and over my arm. I tuck him under my wing so he can have a proper snooze till we arrive in town. How I love the sweetness of that moment.

20

I wonder how life would have been if I'd had a real mother and not one who was too young to share her life with me? I still have so much to learn. I've read about what home should be. Some say it's a place where you feel warm and never need to question if you are welcome.

I think it doesn't have to be a place. It can be a person who opens their arms to you when you run to them and who actually listens when you tell them things. One who notices that tear that refuses to drop but is there in your voice.

And in between times, home could be like Delia's. Just carry it around with you in your mind. Furnish it with vases of pansies and sloppy dog kisses until you find a place you want to settle.

21

It's dark already as I open Ruby's front door and ease myself in. She's in the kitchen making something with nutmeg in it. I always love that smell, even more after I heard it was an aphrodisiac. I wonder who decided to use the shells as ground cover around the blossoming bougainvilleas at the waterfront. Whoever it was deserves a raise and a big hug.

"That you?" Ruby calls.

"It all depends!" I tease.

"Good! I need to talk to you. I hope you have a minute."

"I do. I have all night." Entering the fragrant kitchen, I sigh. "Is that for dinner? I hope so!"

Ruby turns from the stove and I see right away that she is shaken. She drops the spoon she is using on the floor and the paper towel roll falls in the sink. "Darn! Sorry."

I pick the roll out of the sink and begin to clean the spatter. "No worries, what's up?"

I notice a woman seated at the table. Her hands are folded as if in prayer, but she is looking directly at me.

Ruby's eyes dart at her and back to me. "Sorry, Dolores, this is Jade. Jade, Dolores. Sit down a minute, Sweetie."

Jade puts out her hand and we touch briefly. She is dark skinned, and a woman—as they say—of size. She wears a black sweat suit and her hair is pulled back into an ample bun. Her only concession to fashion is a large ring in her left eyebrow, studded with one red stone. Her smile is quick and genuine.

I recognize the large bubbling sound from the huge pot on the stove. Anything that big and boiling in the kitchen is "oil-down," a stew with every possible good thing added—from pig snout to chicken dumplings to salt meat to callaloo, breadfruit, and vegetables, and covered over with coconut milk. Simmer it all day.

But why today? This is way too much for three people. This is a company dish. I know that to be true. So I sit down with questions all over my body and little spasms of shivers up my back.

"What's going on, Ruby?"

Ruby moves around to the empty chair and sits down.

"I'm going to need you to trust me, Dolores. You know I care about you, right? I mean since you came here just a few days ago, I feel that we are meant to be friends. Do you feel that?"

I nod my head, yes. Anyone should know by now that this is not the way I want to find a friend. I feel like I'm going to die of panic. If I could run away I would, but I'm held onto my chair by invisible hands gripping my shoulders.

"Will you trust me? Do as I ask and not question me?"

"What's in your arsenal?" Holly had asked me. "What do you have to keep yourself safe and to take care of you?"

I had pointed to my counselor, my doctor, my new friends in the Recovery Center. Now I knew what she was getting at. All those I mentioned were people around me, like my circle of support. What she really wanted to know was what did I have inside me that I could count on when things went sideways.

What do I have to work with now, at this table, with Ruby and Jade's dark eyes penetrating mine?

All my protecting angels are screaming at me. "No! Get up. Leave. Go to the airport and sleep there in a chair till your flight takes off. Look down on this island through the clouds and smile and wave goodbye. Save yourself, dammit, don't fall for this. You'll be so sorry."

"Can you trust us this one time?" Jade says as she reaches for my hand across the table. I look at their tired brown faces and their searching eyes.

"Yes," I say. And then I say it again. "Yes."

The next hour is filled with packing the hot oil-down into metal coffee cans and wrapping the nutmeg sweet bread and fruit in foil and placing it all into black garbage bags. We gather our belongings and put them in a steamer trunk in Ruby's room and leave the house. Apparently we are not heading for big city lights. For the first time, I see Ruby lock the front door and turn out the porch lamp.

We turn down the pathway to the dock.

When we get there, Jade bends to feel for a rope attached to a wooden rowboat under the dock. She moves back on her knees a few feet and tries again. A metallic sound comes from the metal bow ring under the weathered boards and each of us inhales sharply. Sounds like this are common at the water front until you create them yourself.

Then they become like signals. We freeze for several moments and then she tries again.

"Got it. Here, hold the rope until I get up," her voice is raspy and tired.

Pulling it out into open water is easy, but it takes a good deal of maneuvering to get the three of us seated into the wooden boat. With the coffee cans full of hot oil-down and the foil wrapped bread, we struggle to balance the dinghy.

Ruby has settled at the middle of the craft in order to ply the oars. So we are not just delivering food to the boat. We are taking the boat somewhere in the dark of night with just a sliver of moon already sunk to the west.

I had agreed to come. I had agreed not to question. But now I am ready to renege on all the stupid promises I had ever made in my life. And there had been plenty.

Ruby and Jade are bundling their jackets around themselves so I do the same, the whole time wishing that I had brought a sleeping bag and a big bottle of sleeping pills. I don't swim well. Besides, I am terrified of what might be in the black water right below us sending little tendrils up the side of the creaky boat or baring its saber teeth to bite a hole in the bottom.

As we move slowly away from the land—my cue for my breath to stop entirely—I feel the certainty of cold water on my toes. This can't be. Ruby and Jade are bringing all three of us out to the middle of the sea in a leaky boat. Now what? Somebody's going to break out the popcorn and a deck of cards and we sail on till morning?

No. No popcorn. I watch as Jade reaches around Ruby, who is rhythmically rowing in the center seat, and hands me an empty plastic container the size of a child's sand bucket. She says, "Bail and don't stop!"

By this time, I have big tears running down and off my chin. I swallow my sobs, and when I can't I pretend to cough. But I keep on bailing, finally catching the rhythm of the oars, which together bring several tunes to mind that I remember from childhood. I almost put myself into a hypnotic trance, which keeps me from screaming the songs out loud.

22

I stare at the sea as I bail. The night opens me to eclectic thought journeys. Am I the first to figure out so clearly the nature of water, and it being vastly diverse, almost at odds with itself, and even showing human characteristics? How do I explain? I mean, the sheer light mists that hang over the sea in the morning don't compare at all with a roaring waterfall or the still dark waters of a rain forest pool. They're both water, but they are so different. And ocean water itself is so unwelcoming to the non-swimmer, but not to the triathlon competitor who seeks it out and embraces it as an old friend. My wading into the gentle rolling surf at the sand beach with Mariposa was fun and always a game of catch and chase. The sight of a sundown pageant of clouds and breakers always filled me with moments of pure awe. But here, crossing the wildness in the dark of night, I am totally aware that the sea water holds the possibility of violence and probably my own death.

My mind is jammed full of memories and voices. Holly's voice was saying something about the lens we look through. We all have a personal lens, crafted from who we are and what has happened to us in our lives. Our hopes and even our losses are tied up in how we experience life. She said it was good to know that.

I remember as a teenager standing behind yellow police barricade tape in Houston with a crowd of curious others to watch a nine-story building come down. We waited hours before the planned explosions came, lighting up the darkening sky with ominous flashes. All of us there were stunned to watch the century old building that had been the place for the elite shakers of the city to hold their galas and meetings, and where the governors held forth, and fashion was birthed. It came down after just a few seconds of implosion.

As I watched, I allowed myself to embroider the orange dust clouds with gemstones and glitter from the past, ball gowns and champagne bubbles, and then it settled and was gone. The crowd cheered. The reality of the roof tumbling through the lower floors, the outer walls that had been the face of the classic space for a century caving inward in like a wet cardboard box, made me cry. I cried right there on the street with a hundred people watching. I remember being angry and disappointed and looking for something or someone to blame.

Whatever was lost that night would live in people's memory. For some, it was the once in a lifetime excitement of seeing a building blown to smithereens. For others, it was an engineering marvel they would tell others about seeing for years. For city facility workers, it was the mess they would be cleaning up for months to come. For the mother, it would be the boom that woke the colicky baby just after it had fallen asleep. For me, it was the melancholy of something lost forever—the disappearance of a physical structure, the inability to hold on one more day. Gone. Like Holly said, different lenses.

Still dipping the little bucket into the bottom of the boat, I see the stars circle us and the occasional meteor fly across. Bail. Throughout the long night I become a machine with moving parts, a companion piece to Ruby's rhythmic oars and Jade's navigating eye. Bail. The boat is never empty of water, but it doesn't seem to get any higher either. They have done this before—Ruby and Jade—I think. Many times. I'll be all right. We'll all be fine. We'll laugh about this in the morning. Besides, if not, what better way to go, right? Bail.

23

Dark shapes fade as we move further away from the island. The hours pass. We are becalmed, and then a swell of waves—I count seven—put us nearly over, and then a calmness where I can hear the oars again. That goes on all night. My childhood songs rise with every swell. *Frere Jacque* sits to my left and *Bingo Was His Name-o* is to my right. Exhaustion overtakes us all.

Finally, I sight black mounds of mangroves in the distance that disappear if I look directly at them. Eventually their submerged roots are scraping our little boat, first one side, then with Ruby's skilled directing the pointed bow slips in between the next two. Bumps to the bottom and shifts to the side are scary warnings as we come closer to a rocky shore. The mangrove branches and roots that are determined to overturn us in the blackness slowly begin to open up. We enter a sheltered cove and Jade sidles us up to a boulder and jumps out toward the rocks. A wet landing.

She drags us by thick rope through waist deep water. I can hear her searching for a place to tie up. Finally, Ruby and I crawl out and push the dinghy until it is stuck between the lava rocks. Still in silence, we pick up the food containers and bags and follow Ruby to a dry spot. Only then does she say we are safe from the venomous sea snakes, but we need to be careful of the landed coral snakes that seek their prey among the vines in the cooler nights.

I become obsessed with the thought of getting out of here. The prospect of returning to the big island the next night with the leaky boat, the sea snakes, and the chance of a storm building up, torture my whole body from my head to my soggy shoes. This is not fair. I cancelled my plane ticket in the confusion of our talk at the kitchen table at the inn. I lost my ability to say no again. I was back to trying to be something I wasn't, by saying I would help them on this one thing. I went right back to the old Dolores. "Sure, I can do that, what is it?"

We pack everything in for over an hour, around fat buttress trees and through hanging vines that trip and hold us. All the while I am reasonably sure that we are annoying the night coral snakes.

Our arrival at our destination has to be explained to me. Before us is a small low building the size of a covered breezeway. It is made of rounded river rocks. It has one door made of wood planks and a narrow slot of a window in each of the four walls. Vines grow up the outside so that it is hard to distinguish from the thick foliage even in the faint light of dawn.

Inside, Jade lights a candle as we drag through the door. In the shadows I detect several cots along the walls, a table and two rough-hewn benches, a fireplace, and a cupboard with three shelves. The shelves hold an odd jumble of items related to cooking and eating. It feels as though we have fallen down a hole onto the page of a children's book about a burrowing family of woodchucks.

Our work in the stone hut starts right away. I'm asked to go back into the rain forest to pick up kindling that is dry enough to burn. This sends a shudder through me. How can I get out of this task without appearing to be the coward that I essentially am? A plastic garbage bag would be my only defense against any predators that are out. I think of the snakes resting among the down branches, so quick in their dash from slither to bite. I can't do this. I need a bathroom with a door to close where I can sit and hide my terror. Then I realize there is no bathroom here. At all.

I want to die right here in the doorway but Jade comes behind me and says, "We'll go together. That's always better."

She then whispers to me about the boat that is to arrive. There are four women this time, she has heard. We need to be at the edge of the island where we landed, on time, in order for the women to swim ashore from a distance of ten or so meters. We cannot speak throughout the whole ordeal. We are simply too close to the mainland of South America where the rescues originate and there is no saying whether armed bounty hunters are not on their way to seize the escaped women. Their fate then would be to go back to imprisonment and severe punishment or to be shot right there to ensure their silence.

Inside, a low fire makes it possible to keep the food safe and warm on the stone shelf at the back above the grate. The nutmeg bread is put in a lidded tin box. Then we each sit on a bed and go over the rules again. Slowly my understanding of our mission comes within my grasp. I might not have come at all out of fear and cold feet if they had been honest back at the inn. It all seems overwhelming to me, but I am here and there is no stopping now.

The lightening sky breaks apart and the rain comes in sheets, hitting the building and finally oozing up from the soaked ground and under our door, creating a mud mire inside. I pull my feet up onto the cot and curl up like a feral cat and sleep through the rest of the daylight.

24

I wake to Jade shaking my shoulder. "It's time, Dolores. Gather the blankets. We don't know what we're gettin' into from this point on. Don't forget flip flops and both blankets."

Ruby is stoking the fire, keeping it low, breaking a limb in half and adding it to the side to dry out. Little sparks like orange fireflies swarm toward the flue pipe leading to the outside. It is still raining but we have to go. The boat is coming and we must be there to receive the live cargo.

The way back to where our canoe is stashed doesn't seem familiar to me. New downed trees cross the pathway and there are rushing streams where I'm sure we had walked on dry land before. I try to put my feet down firmly and lean forward like Ruby and Jade. Somehow it gives me more courage when I tromp down heavily and grip my jaw tight. I still tremble in fear though and forget to breathe.

I hear the waves hitting the rocks and catch a tiny beacon of light out beyond the breakers. It's the fisherman and his dinghy, stopped at the edge of the fog. Ruby holds up her small kerosene lantern. We hear two distinct splashes of bodies jumping into the water and then quietly folding into the tidal waves toward us. Ruby swings the lantern back and forth to keep the swimmers on course. There is not a sound except that of the fisherman dragging his tarp back aboard. We stand breathless as his gas lamp fades out beyond the fog. Everyone involved in this critical moment holds each of our lives in unspoken trust.

I can't remember a more perfect time of strangers being in tune.

It's like a ballet where everyone is on and off the stage at the right time and everyone who leaps through the air is caught.

We embrace the two women and help them up over the rocks, fit them with flip flops, and blanket them for the next part of their journey. There were to be four women. What happed to the other two? Why aren't they here with us? Why does no one mention them? A novice in this unfolding drama, I am learning not to agitate the fragile moment with questions. Focus on the two who have made it this far. Give them everything you have. And we turn and start back to shelter, silently, slow and measured.

25

The stories don't come alive until much later. We put the rich oil-down stew in mugs on the table along with the bread and fresh water. We realize that although they are a day or so without food, they are not be able to ingest much. It's there if they can eat it.

I learn that my agenda is secondary to their needs, and their needs affect every part of their bodies and their souls. We show them the cots, and as they sleep, we sit on planks on the mud floor and watch over them like new mothers. I even have the notion to place a mirror under their noses occasionally just to see if there is breath in the silence.

Over the hours of waiting I learn what their lives have been like up to the moment the tarp covered fishing boat dropped them into the sea just beyond us. But it isn't until the nervousness of getting them to the rough stone hut is past and we are watching them sleep that I feel my heart breaking into pieces. How did I never know about all this?

For twenty-seven years I thought I had experienced every indignity and suffered every sadness a person could in this life. I had a mother who left me with strangers, mixing my early life up with people who took me in just so I wouldn't be out in the weather. Schools that didn't see through my shell, counselors who sat on the other side of their desks— except for Holly—all dictating with their text book vocabulary what I had but never touching me with what I could do about it. It wasn't my fault, any of it. My story had worked against me for all those years, until this night. These two young lives have been objectified and turned into chattel, commodities for the financial and physical pleasure of callous and brutal others.

Reading their sleeping faces is impossible. They are children. They are children who have been sold and bought and borrowed and used and threatened and abused by all those whom they came in contact with. In the flicker of candlelight, they are children. How is this allowed to happen? Where are the defenders?

Oddly, I think of Delia the snail. She had a natural self defense. She had a camouflage and would look like a rock if necessary. She could make a door to keep the water out.

Talons, speed, incisors, burrows, all animals have a means of defense. But how do we humans shield ourselves from the depravity of other humans? Without the understanding that not all humans are good we will always be fooled and coerced. Our young people will be groomed, lied to, and carried away by the promises of those who will abuse them for their own purposes.

26

Light creeps through the slit openings in the walls of our shelter, beckoning us all from our various stages of sleep. Now comes the delicate task of gaining the trust of our weary sojourners.

The stories begin slowly. The mischief maker who is Lita has never tired of riding bicycles with her friends in summer. Their destination would be the foothills of Mt. Jefferson for mud riding. That, of course, brought them home late, buoyant, and so covered in muck that they had to use the garden hose to rinse off before they could enter their homes for a shower.

She got a job at fifteen dressing as a hotdog to stand on the sidewalk and usher customers in to the Coney Island Grille. She studied intermittently for biology class. But she really dug creative writing and the theater class that would culminate in her singing in a quartet in the school musical the June that she was a junior. Even when she became pregnant and had to drop out of high school, she had plans to go back and finish. It would be one year late but she had made plans that would dovetail for her and her baby that would be rich and filled with adventure.

But when little Jack arrived, her friends fell away. They were all still in town but their connection faded like their memories of the fun baby shower they had held for her with the silly games and prizes. Neither of Lita's parents, who were separated, could help with expenses and she felt a passive message from them that this was her mess not theirs. Nineteen now, she is so gaunt that I wonder how she is able to stand. Her dark eyes are dim and her teeth are black.

She had been targeted by a pimp who got to know her through her new job at a store in town. He was older by ten years. He praised her and expressed regrets about how her "fresh beauty" was being wasted in that little town. Promising her a modeling job he was able to tempt her to go with him and to leave Jack with her older cousin until she could make a home for him. It wouldn't take long, months maybe. Then she could bring Jack to a house like she had seen in *People Magazine*, with a pool and a green lawn. Her success would be lauded by entertainment news. Her groomer's promises were soft and coated with sweet deception.

Pimps are good at that. They live in the now of their need and their need is for them alone.

She had heard all the aspirational testimonies from those who stood on the winners' pedestals, the gold medalists and the victorious teams. She had read about the actresses who'd come from being cashiers in Kroger's to become stars, and that scrubby garage band that now waved a Grammy on stage. She had not only heard but she had believed. They had called it the "American Dream." And so it didn't take a great leap of faith to believe his promises.

Having been trapped in human trafficking for almost three years, she figures she has been raped over one thousand times by men of all ages, all lines of work, and all appetites.

Rose fills in bits of her story of being mistreated as a child and sexually abused by her brothers. Her mother and father were heavily involved in their own addictions, giving Rose no safe options.

She had no one. Her attraction to a gang outside Philadelphia was almost preordained. Her tiny athletic body, wiry black hair, and smiling brown eyes would stand out anywhere, and did. At thirteen she was picked up and treated like a princess, until she climbed into a van one night in October of her fifteenth year and was whisked away onto the turnpike headed west then south. Then gone.

All of the next two years were filled with exploitation. She was bartered, traded, and sold.

Sweet Jesus, that could have been me. We both have wounded selves that never received the oxygen of a hug freely given. She had no one to tell her that her body was her own or that she was precious as she was.

I look around the table at the five of us—two worn and in pain and desperately frail, and three of us fighting tears at the grotesque design that has brought us together.

As we gather with mugs of stew and bread, I feel an odd surge fill my chest. I close my eyes, take a deep breath, and put my hands out flat on the table in front of me. My hands are immediately grasped and when I open my eyes there is a circle of touching. I try to name the feeling of this night that trust is born. It is more than a connection. It is a combining of our individual spirits into a sort of benevolent oneness. It is a blessing beyond anything I have ever experienced.

27

Talking is past, now. We sleep the few hours we have before our next move.

Deep into the night there is a stirring. Ruby is packing bread for our guests' next journey. Slipping into shoes and flip flops, and pulling on what wraps we have, we open the wooden door to the quiet blackness. Tree frogs chirping is the only sound I can detect as we follow again in a single file the mile or so to the water.

The tree frogs are a good cover for when we trip or step on a down branch. Their tiny bodies have the ability to close their nostrils and push air from their lungs over their vocal chords. Then the air inflates a sac under their chin. They have been compared to the sound of a full out jackhammer. All that noise from a frog that can balance on my fingertip. A musical marvel just to call a mate to produce more tiny frogs as well as helping to smother the sound of young sex trafficked women trekking slowly to safety. My heart fills with emotion as we reach the rock shore and see a blurry light drifting closer. I am breathless as Lita and Rose hug each of us goodbye and wade toward the light.

Holly's words echo in my mind again. "Think back to a time you felt happy, when you weren't thinking about sad things and weren't lonesome or depressed. That feeling is yours."

I had found that elation many times in the last week, but this early dawn is different. I am full of joy for the liberation that is about to happen for Lita and Rose, yet, I am concerned for the danger they still face. And though it is with some pride that I have been trusted by Ruby and Jade to assist in this part of the rescue, there is uncertainty as to whether I can ever be more than a follower in such a calling. Could I ever do this alone?

I'm sad that we will not see Lita and Rose to their final success. But we have done something good! On second thought, there is not one negative thing that has happened in these two scary days and nights. We just did what we could do, dammit!

"That was so good!" I shout.

Ruby and Jade laugh and put their arms around me as we walk back to the hut to gather our things and clean up for the next time.

We shovel out the fireplace and sweep the ashes out into the forest. We try to make it look as though no one has been here for an age. We wash the mugs out in a fresh stream along with the spoons and stack them dry back onto the wooden shelves. The cots with their thin mattress made of thatch are shaken. There is no food to take back, but there is water in the jugs which we keep for the long trip across the water.

Ruby seems somewhat tentative when she says, "I thought while it's light, we could have a little look around. We'll be leaving at sundown."

Jade sits on one of the benches. She looks weary. "You all go ahead. I'll write some in the journal before I forget the details."

Ruby and I leave her there in the quiet and go out into the dappled sunlight. It's incredibly beautiful. I hadn't noticed the giant leaves that hang down from the philodendron vine. They must be two feet long. I think of the one that Nama had babied on her living room mantel in Random and how she plucked and poked at it to entwine a ceramic statue of Mary. The flowering trumpet vines are blooming pink and salmon, in circles around a big tamarind tree.

We walk around back and Ruby says, "You know, I wasn't sure how this would turn out for you. Seems like it couldn't have been better."

"You and Jade didn't give me much time to think about it," I say. "Five more minutes and I'd have been packing for the States."

"Well, I'm really glad you came. You know I just have something I wanted to mention. I wasn't sure how you'd take it, but—"

"After these two days I think I can take whatever you dish out."

She goes on. "We actually call this a station, like the Underground Railroad was for black slaves who escaped from plantations in the states. It's been here a long time. It must be thirty years or so. It was started by trafficked women. There was a continual trail of women and men brought here in dark nights just as we did this time. I feel like you understand now that you've met Lita and Rose."

"You can hear about it and think you know, but I don't ever think I'll be the same person after this," I say.

"Jade and I were in on the first years of its forming. We helped out pretty much from the beginning. And we got to know some of the women, or girls I should say. Anyway, when you told me your story I thought back and remembered a girl named Angel. She'd had a baby that she'd left on the island when she was taken, a little girl. After three or four years she was one of the ones that escaped."

Ruby whispers now. "She died of pneumonia. Like so many she seems to have lost her immunity from a forced lifestyle of alcohol, poor nutrition, and the abuse. But while she lived, she fought. She was here and she helped make this place."

I walk over to the stone hut and lean against the wall. It starts to rain. So natural here, the rain. Plants adapt to the abundance of water with their long leaf tips. Orchids and bromeliads cling to the trunks of the canopy trees. I can see them as they rise. No need for soil, just a willing partner to assist in their reaching for the light above. A silent compliance between species.

28

I am living on the big island now. I've partnered with Ruby and Jade for five years. As it turns out, Angel was my mother. I have found the elusive pieces of her life and placed them in a jagged array like a story board in my mind.

I have learned that Angel was the nickname she had since birth. Angela was on her birth certificate. Her red hair and freckled nose gave her the appearance of a pixie. I wish I had pinned Nama down and demanded answers. But that was then. When I asked about grandpa, or my mother, or even about Nama herself, I got the stinky eye and silence.

After my life began to calm here, I decided that I had to find what I could. I wasn't going to allow myself any more regrets. Shedding the 'what if's' is an ongoing task for me. As each one leaves, I feel a new freedom of ownership of my life, my decisions, my connections, my 'taking-ons' and my 'letting goes.' What's the worst that can happen, I ask myself now, then deal with it.

I had thought it was futile attempt to try to fill in the empty spaces about my mother, but small towns and islands have networks, I learned, and my story began to change with each question.

I wrote an open letter to the Random Unified School District, hoping for something—anything—to confirm who I was. I received an email from Angel's homeroom teacher in her freshman year of high school. Angel must have been fourteen.

It read:

"You couldn't see Angel and not be attracted to her. But to know her was even more compelling. She had such spunk. Living out there in such a remote area of the county, no siblings at home, she created her own community of friends, all imaginary, except for the animals she took care of.

"I asked the others who were teaching at the time and who remember her, and it's all the same reaction. They remember her fondly and they said they were saddened when she started to associate with kids from out of town. But there was nothing they felt they could do. It seemed to happen so fast at the end of her sophomore year and then she was gone. The story was that she was pregnant and her parents sent her to an island where her sister and her boyfriend had gone to live.

"Since I've retired, I think back on all the kids I worked with and I realize I could have been more of an influence on them personally. Angel is one. I had a bad feeling about her friendships and how easily she trusted. I shouldn't say this but I believed then and still do that she got herself in with a bad bunch of people who promised her the moon and suddenly she was trapped. She never came back to visit. I never heard whether she had the baby.

I'm sorry. I'm not much help.

Sincerely, Mary Jacobs."

I couldn't have asked for more. The gaps are still filling in. I could probably change some of the particulars as they come my way, but the story is there in vivid color and it's mine!

Every morning that we arrive on the rocky shore of Angel Station with our food and water and wait through the night for the boat to arrive, it is a different heart thumping experience. My joy is in seeing it all work smoothly for the young people who silently pass through. I have no doubt this is where I should be.

I am putting together a circle of rocks, some jagged and hard from the lava tunnels at the base of the volcanic mountain, and others I brought from the shore, polished by the tides. Soon it will work its way around the entire area where our stone shelter stands. It will be here to remind us of who we are inside and what we can do when we let go of our fears.

A Note from the Author

I remember as a child being first unbelieving and then horrified as I learned of slavery in our country's history. I soon learned it still exists, from migrant worker bondage, to concentration camps at our borders, to human trafficking and sex trafficking of adults and children. I want to witness with my life and words against this tyranny.

> You may choose to look the other way
> but you can never say again
> that you did not know.
>
> *William Wilberforce*

Study Guide

For use with addiction, mental health, and life coaching sessions, there is a study guide available.

Contact Ginger Rankin at gingerrankin@moscow.com

Acknowledgements

Thanks to Sue Fitzmaurice at Rebel Magic Books, for her encouragement, editing, and publishing of my book with great care and persistence. She has a special way of understanding where I am and where I want to be in my story.

And thanks to David for reading my manuscript—more than once. I appreciate his honesty, his knowledge, and his endless patience.

About the Author

Ginger Rankin is originally from Pittsburgh, Pennsylvania. She is a mom, a grandmother, a dog lover, a middle school teacher and married to her best friend, David.

She lived and worked for two years on Spice Island in the Caribbean and fell in love with the country and its people.

She and David now live on the Palouse in north Idaho.

Grapefruit Parlor

REBEL MAGIC

www.rebelmagicbooks.com

Made in the USA
Las Vegas, NV
15 February 2024